FIRST ST(

First Story changes lives through writing.

We believe that writing can transform lives, and that there is dignity and power in every young person's story.

First Story brings talented, professional writers into secondary schools serving low-income communities to work with teachers and students to foster creativity and communication skills. By helping students find their voices through intensive, fun programmes, First Story raises aspirations and gives students the skills and confidence to achieve them.

For more information and details of how to support First Story, see www.firststory.org.uk or contact us at info@firststory.org.uk.

Click to Add Title
ISBN 978-0-85748-179-5

Published by First Story Limited
www.firststory.org.uk
Sixth Floor
2 Seething Lane
London
EC3N 4AT

Typesetting: Avon DataSet Ltd
Cover Illustration: Muzzi Khomusi
Cover Design: Dipa Mistry
Printed in the UK by Intype Libra Ltd

Click to Add Title

An Anthology

By The First Story Group
At Babington Community Technology College

Edited and introduced by John Berkavitch | 2015

FIRST STORY
Creativity Literacy Confidence

As Patron of First Story I am delighted that it continues to foster and inspire the creativity and talent of young people in challenging secondary schools.

I firmly believe that nurturing a passion for reading and writing is vital to the health of our country. I am therefore greatly encouraged to know that young people in this school – and across the country – have been meeting each week throughout the year in order to write together.

I send my warmest congratulations to everybody who is published in this anthology.

HRH The Duchess of Cornwall

Thank You

Kate Kunac-Tabinor, **Keith Webb** and all the designers at OUP for their overwhelming support for First Story, and **Dipa Mistry** specifically for giving her time to design this anthology.

Muzzi Khomusi for illustrating the cover of this anthology.

Melanie Curtis at **Avon DataSet** for her overwhelming support for First Story and for giving her time in typesetting this anthology.

Intype Libra for printing this anthology at a discounted rate; **Tony Chapman** and **Moya Birchall** at Intype Libra for their advice.

The Dulverton Trust and **Trusthouse Charitable Trust** who supported First Story in this school.

HRH The Duchess of Cornwall, Patron of First Story.

The Trustees of First Story:
Ed Baden-Powell, Beth Colocci, Sophie Dalling, Charlotte Hogg, Sue Horner, Rob Ind, Andrea Minton Beddoes, John Rendel, Alastair Ruxton, Mayowa Sofekun, David Stephens and Betsy Tobin.

The Advisory Board of First Story:
Andrew Adonis, Julian Barnes, Jamie Byng, Alex Clark, Julia Cleverdon, Andrew Cowan, Jonathan Dimbleby, Mark Haddon, Simon Jenkins, Derek Johns, Andrew Kidd, Rona Kiley, Chris Patten, Kevin Prunty, Zadie Smith, William Waldegrave and Brett Wigdortz.

Thanks to:
Arts Council England, Authors' Licensing and Collecting Society, Jane and Peter Aitken, Tim Bevan and Amy Gadney, Suzanne Brais and Stefan Green, Boots Charitable Trust, the Boutell Bequest, Clifford Chance Foundation, Clore Duffield Foundation, Beth and

Michele Colocci, the Danego Charitable Trust, the Dulverton Trust, the Drue Heinz Trust, Edwin Fox Foundation, Gerald Fox, Esmée Fairbairn Foundation, the Thomas Farr Charity, the First Story Events Committee, the First Story First Editions Club, the Robert Gavron Charitable Trust, the Girdlers' Company Charitable Trust, Give a Book, the Golden Bottle Trust, Goldman Sachs Gives, the Goldsmiths' Company Charity, Kate Harris, the Laura Kinsella Foundation, Kate Kunac-Tabinor, the Lake House Charitable Foundation, John Lyon's Charity, Sir George Martin Trust, Mercers' Company Charitable Foundation, Michael Morpurgo, Old Possum's Practical Trust, Oxford University Press, Philip Pullman, the Pitt Rivers Museum, Psycle Interactive, Laurel and John Rafter, the Sigrid Rausing Trust, Clare Reihill, the Royal Society of Literature, Santander, Neil and Alison Seaton, the Staples Trust, Teach First, the Francis Terry Foundation, Betsy Tobin and Peter Sands, the Trusthouse Charitable Foundation, University College Oxford, Garfield Weston Foundation, Caroline and William Waldegrave, and Walker Books.

Most importantly we would like to thank the students, teachers and writers who have worked so hard to make First Story a success this year, as well as the many individuals and organisations (including those we may have omitted to name) who have given their generous time, support and advice.

Contents

Foreword

At Babington Community College, we celebrate our diversity. We all have different histories and have been on very different journeys. Each of us will find pieces of work in this collection that speak to us. We might admire the beauty of the images in one poem, the honesty in another, or the wittiness of a short story.

We should celebrate that so many Babington students were willing to share their ideas with a public audience. Working with such creative students on this book has been a real privilege. It's been a genuine collaboration and as an English teacher at Babington, I'm exceptionally proud to have so many different contributors to the anthology. After all, everyone has a poem or story inside of them, don't they?

Everyone who worked on the project was of equal importance to its eventual success, so no one got to decide on a definitive title. Rather, let's let the reader decide what the work means to them.

Thanks for reading,

Ed Herbert
A very proud English teacher

Foreword

It is a real pleasure to have some words of my own included alongside the varied and stimulating work of our talented students.

All the work produced has been written outside lesson time, which means the old-fashioned value of writing for pleasure is intact in the age of the MP3 player and Xbox. As ever I am full of admiration for the quality of the work produced by our students – but even more impressive has been the way they have worked so hard to improve their initial pieces. That is the true value of this project.

Our students have not only had the chance to work with a professional writer, but also to learn about the craft of writing. There are many more words left to be written in the English language. It would be nice to think that some will be written by our students.

Mark Penfold

Introduction

John Berkavitch

WRITER-IN-RESIDENCE

Working with First Story at Babington has been an incredible experience.

Over the course of the last year I have been lucky enough to be part of something genuinely life-changing.

During this time I've seen a love of words transform people. I've witnessed poetry win hearts and change minds. I watched stories breathe new perspectives into old opinions. And along the way I remembered the real reason why I wanted to be a writer.

Over the last year an incredibly talented group of young people, stemming from a wide range of cultures and backgrounds, came together in a supportive network of creativity that has helped unlock their potential to express who they truly are.

I have been honestly moved by what some of the writers I have worked with have been able to achieve as a direct result of their involvement with this project.

A process that proves, without a doubt, that everyone has the right to have their voice heard and that every voice is important.

Babington, you've made me feel excited about the future.

Thank you.

Six Words

Saabirin Abdulkadir Sayed

In this world,
Expect the unexpected.

Home

Daniella Southin

Home, an oasis within the blitz,
My table, a lagoon in the desert,
My door, an embrace, an escape from the hostility,
My mirror, an illusion, a deception from the truth.
My tears, never forbidden, caught and cradled,
My heart, protected from the horror beyond,
Me, embraced amongst the forgotten,
Home, love within the abandonment.

Metaphor World

Simon Robinson

Life is the sky,
Seemingly never-ending,
Things softly declining,
The light is the sun,
The ever-expanding darkness,
She was the moon,
Smaller, slimmer but still,
As important as the sun,
Death is the night sky,
Beaten by new life,
My bed was a mother,
Waiting with a warm embrace,
My room was a castle,
And I was the king,
The house was a knight,
Standing brave against the enemy,
In this unrelenting world.

I Come From

Megan Lange

I come from fighting over covers,
Ten people in a small house,
I come from an old minivan,
Check for spaces three times,
I come from Primark T-shirts,
Too-baggy jumpers,
I come from checking charity shops first,
Then trying elsewhere,
I come from taped up iPods,
Wearing your shoes until your toes stick out,
I come from hiding in cupboards with books,
The front room's too crowded,
I come from home.

Time

Nicolas Merriman

The past is behind,
The present is now, feel it,
The future is soon.

The Walk

Owen Clark

As I walk through
The infinite maze of life,
The souls of wanderers glow,
The sorrow and hate eating them whole,
The air blood-cold,
Yet we still stand bold.
My hands are wet from the tears I wept,
Still I walk and walk,
Hiding behind a smile.

The pines and leaves brushing by my cheeks,
Clawing and scraping for a touch,
I suppose it does not bother me much,
Yet still I push
And weave my way through,
Pain surrounding me,
Like the air is hounding me,
Holding me down,
Suppressing my ability to fly,
I want to cry,
hiding behind a smile.
The world is a trap – an evil abyss,
The walls, the leaves, the sky, the ground,
It all is an illusion. We suffer from the same delusion,
That is the thing that runs through my mind,
As I stare at a squirrel lying on its behind,

Blood dripping from its septic wound,
I can no longer smile,
For there is no reason to do so,
I lie back, my head staring above,
And see the burning rays of the sun,
How can this ever be classed as fun?

If a life for a life is paid in these times,
And I'm the victim of this brutal crime,
Then why am I on the fiery plains of hell,
Yet I still wander,
And wander and wander,
Hoping to find peace.

When I Was Ten

Seren Pope

I ran down the hill to my friend's party,
The smell of beef and bacon in my nose,
The cool breeze and cold water cooled me down,
Laughing, shouting, music making loud noise,
Jelly, vanilla ice cream, taste gorgeous,
Prizes won from games played in the garden,
The Cherryade fizzes inside my mouth,
Bristly leaves poke my arm as I walk past,
I feel the cold concrete on my bare feet,
I feel the cold concrete on my bare feet.

I Remember

Hibaaq Deria

I remember getting my first detention and thinking it was cool,
Following girls who were the bullies in the school.

Six Words

Rajdeep Dulkoan

Families died in bombings –
Hope didn't.

Up Above

Abdi Gafar

The sky was a blue blanket,
The clouds were white fluffy pillows,
The sky was ocean-like,
The sun was a fireball,
The sun was a yellow volleyball,
The moon was a white balloon,
The sun was a yellow football,
The clouds were blankets in the sky.

Maybe I Come From

Muzzi Khomusi

Maybe I come from a rented flat.
People sitting, waiting for change,
Sitting on a cold bed next to a boot-sale mat.
Some tears, sitting in a takeaway.
Whilst ministries make decisions,
I come from a place in the UK.

I Come From

Bridget Coleman

I come from friendships that span continents,
My school friends, we laugh and smile,
Theirs are probably real but mine is normally fake,
I hide from my family,
Keep my secrets away,
I share a bedroom with a sister, bunk-beds.
Feeling springs through the mattress,
Mould on the walls.
The condensation trickles down to the floor,
I come from a not-rich but not-poor family,
But closer to poor,
All my friends have iPhones or iPads.
But I have a cheap phone from Tesco.
I come from a large international family,
My family doesn't understand me, no one does,
My three sisters are all older, the more mature, the meaner.
My mum and my dad, still happily together,
My mum is from London,
My dad I don't even know.
I live with my dad but he's only there on Mondays,
His brothers and his sisters –
He has nine –
His mum, Bridget Coleman,
I visit her grave but get worried because it's my name too.
I hurt inside but I don't show my heart is shrivelled
But why?

I bury my sorrows with music.
Sometimes it helps but not always,
So why?
I live in Leicester, a run-down city,
Even though what I've said is negative,
I'm positive that it's where I belong.

Spring

Nicolas Merriman

Spring's not forever,
But you shouldn't worry much,
Summer is the best.

The Curious Case

Lucy-Jane Carey

Born an adult,
Died a baby.

The Walk

Seren Pope

Alone in the gloomy forest.
The unnaturally thin trees tower over me,
Blocking out the moonlight,
Only darkness.
Long branches, crowded with leaves, create a shelter above me.
The constant patter of the rain doesn't disturb me.
It's taking forever.
No visible exit.
Darker and darker, nothing I can do.
I hear rustling and I stop.
I look around but nothing.
Just the wind.
My journey along the narrow path continues.
The trees whisper softly.
Finally!
I can see a dim light – it must be the exit.
It has to be. I rush.
My body collides with the ground.
I drag myself back up again and carry on.
A rustling sound.
Just the wind.
I know it's not.
I attempt to run.
Something clutches its arms around me.
I try to escape the tight grip.
It covers my mouth, I can't scream.

No help.
It's a hairy creature, long claws, sharp teeth.
Its hand lunges towards me.
I'm a target and it hits bullseye.
I collapse.
Teeth sink in.
Life taken out.
Weakness.
The creature stops, I crawl away.
Then something clamps my foot.
The creature.
Blood gushing out.
A waterfall on my face.
Pain in my entire body.
A howl.
Loud and clear.
It's not what I think it is.
This is a dream, it has to be.
There's no other explanation.
More pain.
More weakness.
No life.
Just death.

I Want

Megan Lange

I want to have that one day where everything goes right,
I want to cry a storm,
I want to dance in the rain,
I want to be a cloud,
I want to want nothing,
I want to watch the world go by,
I want to not be bothered by the time,
I want to get lost in a library,
I want to lose myself in a book,
I want someone to get embarrassed because I'm watching,
I want it to be a person I get embarrassed around,
I want to run,
I want no one to stop me,
I want to truly feel free,
I want to feel truly free,
I want to be truly alone,
I want to be surrounded by people,
I want the person I care about to say I love you,
I want to say it back,
I want to change the world,
I want to regret nothing.

What Am I?

Megan Lange

I can contain entire planets,
Or tell you more about your world,
I draw you in and you're my willing captive,
Filling your heart with joy,
Then breaking it into pieces,
You know I hurt you,
But you don't want to leave,
I leave you hanging,
But you still wait for more.

Something from Nothing

Muna Farah

Nothing, then something. That's how we all begin, right? From the first breath of life expanding into your lungs. The race has begun, the race to create yourself. A blank canvas becomes beautiful art. Never perfect but always human. You'll grow and plant your mark as the seconds elapse.

Happiness, sadness, surprise, fear, anger and love. All the emotions there ever existed you will feel. Some are unbearable, maybe lethal. And some are astonishing. Fuel a strong desire to forever feel such happiness. Although you don't see it one day your life will time-lapse in front of your very eyes.

I Come From

Usamah Yakub

I come from,
A house with four siblings,
Playing video games and sports,
Shuttles and rackets,
Gliding through water,
My family's helpful advice,
Watching animé,
With my sister,
Eating with delight,
Loving my distant relatives,
But only distantly,
Dreams, aspirations, achievements and goals,
Memories, friends and fun with my family,
School days, education and enemies,
Success and failure,
Remembering to enjoy life,
Memorizing and reciting the Quran,
Learning history,
Living in the present,
Asthma, eczema and all the diseases I wish I never had,
Living in a resort and eating coconuts and sugar cane,
This is what I come from.

My Home in a Power Cut

Bridget Coleman

My cave home makes me blink again and again.
I need light.
Reaching out, searching for the cure to this darkness,
The bathroom, borrowed from a hospital,
Grasping for the light I succeed, I squeeze,
Wetness slips from my hand,
A thud hits the floor at the same time as my soap.
After the sloppy mess, my adventure for light goes on.
I trip, I fall.
The smell of dampness,
The feel of rough sandpaper against my bare skin.
I clutch the air and miss.
My body drags itself and climbs to its feet.
My hand tells me I have found something cold and dusty.
Boldly I grab this creature.
Collapsing to the ground, we fall, feeling nothing.
No pain, but also no feeling of life.
Still no light, the only thing in sight is my younger self,
Happy with my family, I come back to reality, sadly.
Distant photos scattered, too many memories.
My legs move faster and faster,
Escaping this monster called the past.
Risking; that's life, repeatedly knowing where my feet stand
Touching the light, I score the goal.

My eyes are sheets of water washing the hurtful light out.
They turn to waterfalls as my head rushes swimming chaotically
    with the memories.
Not being able to deal with the pain,
Waking up from this nightmare and so fulfilling my destiny,
Escaping, leaving, goodbye forever.

Sky

Eliab Habte

The sky was a light at sea,
The sun was a horse, galloping all day long,
The wind was the road for the eagle,
The clouds were the life of the mountains.

Home

Hibaaq Deria

It was a cold, autumn afternoon. I'd just got back from school.

I walked in through the gate and went towards the bin.

I moved the bin and crouched down to fetch the keys I'd hidden that morning.

That Monday had seemed to be like any other Monday.

Both boring and exhausting, but nothing out of the ordinary.

Just like any other day.

I opened the door and as I went in I was greeted by the heat-rays from the heater that my brother had left on that morning.

I should tell him to turn it off, as it wouldn't be *him* paying the bills.

But he moaned about it being cold, whilst walking round the house without a top and with no socks and no shoes on.

My mother hadn't been at home and the kids were glued to the TV.

That sofa was where they would abide until *Power Rangers Super Megaforce* would end.

And when it finally did end, everything would change.

On the Unit

Morgan Matthews-Read

On the unit I whistle,
In tune with the birds,
Whilst sitting and waiting,
I follow the lead,
Friends with these jacked up mugs,
My parents say I am smoking,
Hanging with the wrong crowd,
I need to be with the birds, they say,
But the eyes follow me around.
Pushing my buttons trying to get me steamed,
Trying to make me blow my top,
Getting me heated,
Wanting me to boil over,
As I anger they flip my feet,
Asking me to repeat,
My friends get scalded.

Six Words

Seren Pope

They always confuse reality,
With dreams.

The Walk

Megan Lange

A swaying in the distance,
A green curtain falls,
I see mossy walls,
As silence wraps around me,
My hand shifts the emerald drape,
As the whirlpool of leaves surrounds me.
The gull's wings speak to me
Up, down, up, down, glide.
Repeating,
Staying the same.
Familiar patterns that never change.
Familiar beating,
Familiar trees,
Familiar wind rushing past,
Familiar grass glistening on the ground,
The scent tickles my nostrils,
The greenery whispers to me,
The fairies beckon.
It's a world waiting, just for me.
This is where I belong.
My wings spread and I join the birds,
Free from my cage at last.

Mutual Change

Saabirin Abdulkadir Sayed

It was a day like any other: same routine, same me. But something happened to me that day which made me view things differently. I recall the first day we met. It was love at first sight. His blue, sapphire eyes, soul-searching and so full of life. I felt as if he could illuminate my empty, dark heart. Each time we met, he slowly broke the bricks that I had built in my heart. It was not a good thing. I didn't want to repeat the same mistake. I was young, foolish, and thought it was love, but as the years went by... we went by. We weren't the same, and the spark we had had fizzled, and I couldn't keep the fire going. I ran out of things to give. We all have to sacrifice something, but at times it can be a good thing. It was a mutual change.

Cat

Lucy-Jane Carey

I grab my pen and paper.
Sitting at my desk I start to draw my cat.
First the head, then the body and face.
Adding eyes, tail, ears and the details of the fur and features.
To my surprise, as I finish colouring,
It seems to lift from the page.
I blink...
And the drawing is gone.

Stuck in Reverse

Bridget Coleman

It begins with my head going backwards.
As if the seat is hugging every part of my body,
To cover me up from this terror,
But it doesn't help.
Pieces of glass fly away from my skin.
It's as if my skin can heal within seconds,
My body looks clean from all the cuts,
The air flows back away from my head,
Glass joins into groups,
Then fuses together.
The cars slowly begin to un-crumple
I am reversing in my car
The other one drifts into the distance.
Rapidly, storming round every corner.
Music gets sucked back into the speakers,
The engine goes,
My key ejects from the hole.
Out of the car,
Into the house,
My day has just begun,
Let's make it a good one.

15 of 100 Needs

Morgan Matthews-Read

1. I need what is needed,
2. I need not to want the unheroic,
3. I need the power to write poems,
4. I need the pieces to my life jigsaw,
5. I need patience for other people,
6. I need to listen to what my peers say,
7.
8. I need to look for a 7th need,
9. I need knowledge because it is 'power',
10. I need more creative ideas,
11. 01001001 00100000 01101110 01100101,
12. I need the motivation to motivate,
13. I need the night shift for a further advance,
14. I need to show my friends revenge,
15. I need to be a rock star.

Family Pets

Zack Thotho

My dad is a stubborn cat,
He treats my mum like a doormat,
My sister is a goldfish.

A Galifreyan Diabetic Love Story

Seren Pope

When you said *hi*,
I flew into your heart of pie.
You gave me diabetes,
Because you're so sweet.
I'm so low,
So it's not safe for me to go.
You regenerate my heart,
Like you're a Doctor.
But I'm from Galifrey,
And there we don't say,
I love you,
We say…

Destiny

Kejti Ismail

Born a king,
Died a soldier.

Gifted

Bridget Coleman

Blind, but can see the future.

I Come From

Nicolas Merriman

I come from a low class neighbourhood,
In a house with high-class values,
I come from tiring, running and lots of food,
I come from hanging up the wet umbrellas,
I come from playing Pokémon cards,
I come from being surrounded by friends,
Most of the time.
I come from lonely summer holidays,
And from awesome happy holidays,
I come from happiness in separation,
I come from not knowing or understanding,
From learning and befriending,
I come from Mensa meetings with friends from school,
I come from all of this and more.

My Home

Iman Egal

My home is a split infinitive,
I'm not really going to expand on this.

Home-Less

Hibaaq Deria

This cardboard was my duvet,
The pavement my pillow,
The people my television,
The roadworks my alarm,
The harmonica my occupation,
The food cart my cuisine,
This ragged coat my pride and joy,
And these passers-by my family.

The Forgiving One

Hibo Deria

I had destroyed her childhood,
Killed her ego, its bleeding remains scattered in the corridors.
Tore through the flimsy veil of confidence that blanketed her,
And tossed away her integrity.
Exposed her darkest secrets,
Abused her both mentally and physically.
Taking her to a state of torment,
With no escape, imprisoned.
Even after all this,
She forgave me.

Roulette

Muzzi Khomusi

Two people,
One bullet,
Your turn.

Home Again

Bridget Coleman

The house was a packed nightclub,
The door is a bouncer I am scared to pass,
The window is a magnifying glass,
Helping me to see all,
The hallway is a tunnel.
It's an oven in the house but I am a freezer,
The stairs are Mount Everest,
My bedroom is a treasure chest,
My bed a magician's sarcophagus.
The bathroom is a pale hospital ward,
But it is the only room safe to unravel dark secrets,
The living room is a stage,
My sister's room a cage, she never leaves.
My parents room a field,
My house to my family is heaven,
To me it is hell.

Haiku

Morgan Matthews-Read

In the coming spring,
The leaves were very crispy,
Good for jumping in.

The Walk

Eliab Habte

The never-ending walk that began with one foot forward.
The tread that defines and changes my fate.
Many outcomes await but only one to be chosen.
What I hear, what I see and what I accept to be real,
They may not be real.
What is this I am feeling?
A shock to the nerves.
It stands in front of me, it causes my hands to be numb,
My blood to escape my skin,
My breath to be as grey as the mist floating like clouds.
Life goes on, all the life around me lives on.
Every day trying to survive.
That innate need to live on, to keep going.
Am I walking to survive?
Is it a need to live on?

I Come From

Muzzi Khomusi

I come from Biryani, textiles and long school years.
I come from *CBeebies*, the laughter, the cheers.
I come from Rowlatts, the pain and the truce.
I come from the fact, the fiction and the news.
I eat from disposable plastic plates,
Cooking on a council stove until late.
I come from the beatings and the bruises and the fights,
The moments that one's eyes would deny.
Living in a rented flat, the room's a mess.
Benefits and low income, I don't dress to impress.
I come from lies, experience and mistakes.
I come from friendship, a mirage of snakes.
I come from the oily Maryland boxes,
Conversing about football, Man U losing to the Foxes.
I come from a mum, who's been beaten and reshaped,
A dad with no mum, no education, no mates.
I come from strive, passion and endeavour,
To make my parents proud, succeed however,
I come from heartbreak, *keep no hope* my dad said.
I come from a dream that cannot be put in words.
Aspirations of success.
I come from grime and rap.
I come from something that is hidden by a gesture,
I come from a place called Leicester.

When I Was Ten

Daniella Southin

The spring when I was ten was typical,
There were friends, family and all my teachers.
My friends laughing, grass tickling, sun gleaming,
Memories were made, good times created.
My mum cooking… to be honest, burning,
Though I knew she was just trying her best.
My teachers nagging, coaching and pushing,
In the end it eventually paid off.
Flowers were blossoming, days turned to nights,
I was maturing and spring was thriving.

Weather

Sarah Adams

Her eyes shone like the sun,
His cried a rainfall,
And his tears,
Made puddles on her ground.

The Walk

Megan Lange

I breathe the fresh air into my lungs, and as I smell the grass I can tell it's been freshly mown. My Converse smother the delicate blades and then leave them alone, to spring back up again as if I had never set foot there. As I leave the lawn behind the grass begins to grow untamed, long and wild. I'm running now, the long green blades tickling my bare ankles as I rush past.

Reaching a clearing, I stop, taking in my surroundings with a long look as I slowly turn around in a circle. I catch my breath. The space is almost a perfect circle, and is enclosed by shrubbery and trees. At the far end there is a curtain of green and when I sweep it aside a cavern is revealed. I shout and I hear my voice echoed back to me like a record on repeat, but this one slowly fades out until I am left once more in eerie silence. I stretch my hands out before me, dreaming of monsters and adventure, but all I reach is walls at the side and emptiness ahead.

I can hear the sane part of my mind shouting; *turn back, turn around, it's dangerous, I'll hurt myself, I'll fall, I'll break my neck, I'll die*. Meanwhile, there's a small background voice whispering away: *go forwards, see what's there, discover something, don't be a coward*.

I step forward.

This House

Daniella Southin

Our home is an album of memories,
Started but never finished.
Their house a handful of tears,
Flooding but always… Bawled, sealed, locked?
My room is my story,
Details of myself scattered across the floor.
Her room is a canvas,
Awaiting a brush.
My home, their house,
Just chests built from bricks.
The treasures are either hidden within or nowhere to be found.

Who Is Darkness?

Nicolas Merriman

Darkness is dark.
He has black hair, clothes, eyes, basically everything.
Even his personality is dark.
He doesn't care about anything or anyone,
And spends his time looking into space, as if in another dimension.
He lives away from everything in the spooky side of town,
As if a cloud is constantly suffocating hope and light.

The Orange Plane

Owen Clark

My halved body covered in burnt skin and fabrics,
Pushes itself back into the ferocious fires.
A fire that latches its orange tentacles onto my body,
Pulling off my burns and repairing my clothes.
My body connects to a piece of metal.
As it pulls upwards,
My body tethers together until I'm perfectly intact.
Staring and screaming at the wound,
Stitching itself together.
Blood is slurped up into my body and I slam back into my chair,
The metal pieces itself together like a jigsaw puzzle.
We glide back
The back end of the plane reconnects until fully intact.
As we glide through the air
I hear the almost alien talk,
Of the stewardess as she struts backwards
Hidden behind closed doors.
'Would you like some tea, sir?'

Seasons

Daniella Southin

Summer to autumn,
From sunshine burning our cheeks,
To leaves on the ground.

Wake Up

Sarah Adams

Your bed is a drug dealer,
Your alarm is the police,
The kettle is my apology.

The Old Man

Bridget Coleman

2014
Home alone, no one to hold,
Thinking of the past and what went wrong.

1973
Shouting, screaming, a bang, silence,
He sat there with his bags, waiting.
I look into his eyes sharp as a needle,
I want to leave but I can't,
I wait, I argue,
I hit, I score,
EMPTY.
Home alone, no one to hold,
What went wrong?

1972
I'm home, I hear…
Crying,
Yet silence.
She is missing, gone,
My baby stolen.
12:00p.m.
A knock,
A light,
Police.
Five minutes later,

She's gone, she's left me.
I can't hold her any more.
I don't have my baby girl.

2014
A bridge,
A step,
That's all.
One prayer,
One shot,
One life,
But mine...
Is over.

The Walk

Guled Ali

My dad and I were strolling across the abandoned avenue, and we were talking about how Britain is suffering from a lot of things. I knew that this conversation was important, but why couldn't we just set off to Maryland and eat a burger?

My dad had never talked about this before. He'd probably been watching too much television. Round the corner was Maryland and I was famished. I finally got to eat something.

I was leaving Maryland when – out of nowhere – there was David Cameron. He was letting the community speak out with their ideas to help the future generation.

I spontaneously leapt towards Mr Cameron and put forward my ideas to him. It was astonishing. I was in front of a camera. I had drops of perspiration coming from my face; I was in front of the media. My father and I mentioned lowering the cost of living and getting the taxes dropped.

Extraordinarily, the press were listening. My father was proud of me. This could be the change of life I wanted. Everyone listening to me – I'm the guy that's been ignored for half my life. I have assurance of the media offering me a good amount of money after what I've done. One day I could be Head of State or part of the Government.

Subsequently I went to the library and people were swarming outside – were already outside the house. I was ecstatic. I could be illustrious at this instant.

I felt like Britain must all know by now. I put my best foot forward, and now I'm on television. David Cameron looked at me and said, 'Everywhere is a walking distance if you have the time.' That statement blew me off my feet; I was stunned by what Mr Cameron had said to me.

The instant Mr Cameron said that, I completely forgot I was on the small screen. Stupidly, I wanted to leave. I couldn't bear the flash of the camera. I was sweating like the River Nile. I was destined to faint soon. What could I do? My dad gave me the stern look not to do anything bad, but I couldn't stay focused.

In a little while, I was going to pull off a prank – if I did, I would certainly be ignored for the rest of my life.

Just before I was going to pull my prank, my dad greeted Mr Cameron and we set off.

Focus

Seren Pope

Eyebrows up,
Duck-face –
The perfect selfie.

A Letter to Myself

Seren Pope

Dear Younger Me,
Remember what we wanted to be?
An artist,
An author,
And a musician too.
These are only a few.
The power to be invincible,
And to be a unicorn.
To be lost in my imagination,
And to be that thorn –
That little thorn that stuck out of the bush.
The little unique one that knows how to be different.
And knows that that's ok.
All these things we know are true.
Yours sincerely,
The Older You.

A Mother's Love

Saabirin Abdulkadir Sayed

Her touch cannot be compared to any other,
As the slightest brush gives you a sensational, loving feeling,
When you're alone in the dark with no one by your side,
She illuminates the room with her smile,
She's the rainbow in the sky that scatters the clouds,
She's like the stars of hope for all the stray souls,
The truest friend who's always by your side,
Whether it's in good times or in times of misery,
A mother's love is tranquil,
There'll be a day where you look back to those days,
When your mother is no longer there.

Haiku

Bridget Coleman

Life doesn't last long,
I will try to live mine well,
As long as I can.

Walking Away

Nicolas Merriman

We appear casual as we leave the scene. Physically strong, but mentally we're frozen, shocked wrecks.

We awkwardly walk along ignoring the bloody stains on each other's shirts.

'Sooo…' I said. My partner, obviously not interested in talking, stays silent. He's shaking and bunching his hands tight.

I can't believe we both made it out. I had saved him, but I guess if it weren't for his brains I wouldn't be here either.

He isn't your typical geek.

'Ermm, where does this package go…?'

He doesn't react. I sigh deeply.

We need to go and wash off these stains but I won't speak to him because I know he won't answer.

He sighs. I take my chance. 'So, that was rough in there, wasn't it?' I say.

He finally replies,

'I don't want to talk about it.'

I Come From

Zack Thotho

I come from a middle class family,
I come from a neighborhood,
I come from watching *Pokémon*,
Marvel cartoons and animé
I come from a father,
And a frustrated mother,
I come from an area full of terraced houses,
I come from a dad who has a complete disregard,
I come from a mum trying to provide,
I come from a restricted fund,
I come from an area full of benefit frauds,
I come from having to share everything with my sister.

The Full Story

Seren Pope

Once upon a time…
The end.

Objectify

Bridget Coleman

Tap, tap, and tap,
Hitting me,
Poking me,
Touching me,
Feeling OCD every time you touch me,
You stop,
Finally,
No…
I am being shaken.

In this small, dark cave, I hop along this tiny path,
Crumbs,
Paper,
Cut, after,
Scrape, after,
My face scarred, it will never leave,
Cuts cover my dented body,
I miss the past,
I still wish I was free.

I used to be so desirable,
I remember sitting with my brothers and sisters,
Growing up and then finding a new home,
Everyone wanted my family, and me,
I've never seen my parents,
None of us did.

I remember us separating,
Them leaving,
Until it was my turn,
My memories are not what they used to be,
I was the chosen one,
I wish I wasn't.

I regret what I said,
It's all my fault,
So now it's karma,
Coming after me for what I did to that girl,
I stopped working and couldn't do what I was made for.

We just couldn't connect like we used to,
She used to care so much,
Keeping me 100% healthy,
I used to be so full of good memories,
Happy holidays,
Dance shows,
It was like she deleted memories from my mind,
Wanting to forget.

I feel that she deserved what she got,
Even though it is a little harsh,
I wish I hadn't said that.

I am so young,
I'm dying,
If only I hadn't ruined her life,
If only I'd fulfilled my destiny,
If only?

Communication Disarray

Hibaaq Deria

In this society,
We're so engrossed in social media,
That we begin to forget the meaningful things in life.
Like speaking face-to-face, instead of from behind screens,
And expressing our emotions, rather than sending emojis.

Just tell us your problems, rather than making it a mystery.
And actually laugh, instead of typing 'LOL' when I say
    something funny.
That's the thing with this society,
We don't do any of these things.
But we can.
By deploying the art of conversation,
And looking up from the very thing that has caused our silence.
By using our voices, to say what needs to be said.
And using our hands,
To paint the picture that needs to be portrayed,
Because in this society there is a communication disarray,
And what better time to set it straight,
Than now.

So, let's learn to coexist, and step away from the things that may
stop this: mobile phone, laptops, and computers, too.

Let's speak and laugh, like we used to.
Now, I know there are some of you out there,
That may not agree with what I have to say.
But I ask you to hear me out,
For what I have to say may be the means for you one day, to
Realise that in this society there is a,
Communication disarray.

Rebel

Ed Herbert

Six word story?
Not my thing, Sir.

WW3

Simon Robinson

World War Three:
Cats vs Dogs!

Illness

Megan Lange

My heart doesn't flutter,
Because it hardly beats,
I don't catch my breath,
Because I barely breathe,
My legs don't shake,
Because I can't walk,
I never hated this,
But you made me want to run,
You made me believe I could fly,
I know it's not much,
It's battered and bruised,
But you can have my heart,
And the rest of me too.

The Question

Bridget Coleman

Will you dance, if I ask?

What I Have Lost

Hibo Deria

What I have lost is bigger than what I have gained,
What I have gained is less than what I have lost,
I am lost in what I have gained,
And I have gained what I have lost.

The Stranger

Seren Pope

The sound of footsteps echoes behind me. I stop, turn around…
nothing. I carry on walking down the narrow alleyway. Footsteps
again! I stop, turn around… nothing. It's all in my head. No! It
must be real! I carry on and then suddenly out of nowhere I feel
a tight grip around me. Pulled down, I feel my fragile body clash
with the concrete floor. I scramble to my feet and I find myself
running out the alleyway and into a busy road. My body, already
damaged by the impact from the floor, gets hit by a colossal metal
object. I cry out. A crowd gathers. A mysterious figure appears
at the back of the crowd. I blink. When I open my eyes again, it's
gone. Then I black out completely.

Shell-Shocked

Nicolas Merriman

My life begins, as I roll away from my birthplace.
A warm, fluffy place now changed for cold, rugged countryside.
This noisy place is full of loud, harsh screeches.
I roll down a ramp, hitting every bump,
And fall onto the dirty floor.
At least I was safe before.
A giant hand grabs me,
I'm bundled in with others of my kind.
I am pushed roughly into the holding pen,
Along with my new acquaintances.
The blackness blinds me and the darkness swallows me.
I yearn for the warmth and comfort of before.
Time passes and my boredom turns to madness.
Finally we stop, and my body is laid across a scale,
Before being forced into the coldest and most horrible situation,
I had ever been in.
It's ten times colder than the countryside.
I can't tell whether my eyes are open or closed.
Luckily I am picked up, and I can see again.
Finally I am warm, then intensely hot, starting to boil.
I am bobbing along, but in my pain I can't enjoy it.
I see death looming above me.
All of a sudden, the knife flashes before my eyes.

Fire

Megan Lange

I watch as the fire flickers.
It dances in the eyes of my fellow campers.
Terror starts to dwindle,
As the fire dies away we run towards it,
The adults urging us on.
The fire starts to gather in one place,
Leaving green trees untouched.
The fire is now concentrated in the centre.
The only other burnt place is a nearby log seat.
Soon this too has healed over, and everything is pristine.
Sitting in a huddle, we tell stories,
Of people who flock to haunted houses after hearing the tales,
And the ghosts get scared off by their presence.
Putting out the fire once the wood has regenerated.
Campers dash into the forest holding it.
Soon after, they return, arms empty.
Bags packed, we run out of the forest,
Excited chatter drifting back into our mouths.
Ready to return home to our normal lives.

The Beauty

Hibaaq Deria

She's beautiful, her edges excite me,
I think she's trying to tell me something,
But won't give me the full picture,
I like the way she announces her fame,
Newspaper reviews, tattooed on her precious skin.

I Remember

Daniella Southin

I remember,
I remember the pain of falling off a swing,
Going to sleep to tales of fairies and Jack Frost,
I remember playing pirates on the cushions of a blue sofa,
Sleepovers with make-up and nail polish,
I remember swaying, a doll with one leg,
My brothers laughed, but my love for her never faltered.
I remember boys with trousers around their ankles.
I remember fun, laughter and love,
I reminisce.

My Home

Nicolas Merriman

My home is my mum holding me with warm arms,
My house is my bike helmet, it keeps me safe,
My house is my dog, loyal and welcoming,
My house is a bombsite.

Born in This World

Saabirin Abdulkadir Sayed

I was born into this world,
I was born this way,
I don't remember her face,
I don't remember her touch.

But I remember her voice,
I remember the nights that they stayed awake,
I felt his kiss.

I was the cause of her pain,
I was the cause of his nerves,
I was the cause of their death.

I am an orphan.

Richard the Third

Mark Penfold

Old bones found,
Back in ground.

Coming Home

Muzzi Khomusi

The front door was the gate to Alcatraz,
Tall, lifeless and unannounced,
The stairs were my fate, a coin toss that reincarnated my emotion,
Then came my corridor, no man's land,
After school I step in cautiously,
My parents' words are bullets that I'd dodge,
The bathroom is a vortex of water and waste,
The burn of morning toothpaste,
Many scenes opened up in the bathroom,
The kitchen was a cat and mousetrap,
My parents cooking was a courtroom,
The storeroom was abandoned and only junk lived there,
Finally my living room, collapsing my limbs.

The Walk

Daniella Southin

Left. Impossible heat scorches my skin,
        Right. My hand strokes my cheek, now sandpaper,
Left. Pain prickles like thorns,
           Right. Barren land swamps my vision,
Left. Squinting against striking light,
         Right. Merely sand awaits me left and right,
Left. Dust intoxicates my lungs,
        Right. Each raspy breath scrapes my throat,
Left. Like nails clawing my neck,
         Right. Oceans of tears distort my vision,
Left. My tongue welcomes the salty droplets,
        Right. But they disintegrate upon touch,
Left. Realisation hits me,
        Right. My last moments brush my fingertips,
Left. I grasp them, drawing them in,
          Right. My soul exposed for relief,
Left everything I cared about behind,
         Right now hope is but a memory,
Left... Nothing is left.

The Match

Nicolas Merriman

At night they play cricket with the moon,
The sky was a great playing field for huge cloudy monsters,
A basketball they play with, brighter than a rocket,
Lots of dotty lights are the spectators in the ground,
The darkness is the anticipation, waiting for the match.

Old Man's Life

Megan Lange

Oh, the joy of birth,
The joy of life,
As they take their first breath,
As they gasp their first laugh,
As they cry their first tears,
As they gulp their first drink,
As they look in your eyes,
As they make you pray they'll be safe,
As they make you feel the old age,
They make you feel content with your life.

What Am I Now?

Megan Lange

I can contain everything or nothing at all,
Some people are gentle and careful,
Others are vicious and angry,
I open up to you,
Bent, crinkled, curled and crippled,
Torn up inside,
Some people leave me blank and empty inside,
Others smother me, filling me with ideas and thoughts,
Some are intricate and detailed,
Others are jumbled and carefree,
I'm useless in water,
And frustrating in high winds,
Parts of me are ancient and faded,
Others are brand new and waiting to be explored,
Some of my personality is copied,
Other bits are wildly original,
Sometimes they tear me up and fold me,
But no matter what,
I am always unique.

Lose My Everything

Iman Egal

I would lose everything just to help you forget the past,
The damage, the tears that your eyes dealt.
You were young, fresh-faced and simple,
You trusted, were abandoned, and missed the warning signals.

'I Love You' was a lie you still haven't come to terms with.
Oh, what I'd lose to protect you, pretend it was an elaborate
    myth,
'An eye for an eye, a tooth for a tooth, a son for a son,'
You refused: to defend him, to save him from being shunned.

I would lose everything I own, my knowledge, my comfort,
To return your life to its true, bright colours,
I would become a black void, an abyss of emptiness,
To soothe you and make sure you don't sleep restlessly.

And I would lose the hand that I write with, as my words are
    redundant.
Nothing I say or write can change fate's hand, no matter how
    abundant,
The shock of what happened must've caused you to unlearn all
    that occurred,
Couldn't tell the difference between reality and fantasy, there's
    a line but it's blurred.

I would lose my sanity if it meant the cancerous monster
    stayed away,
And your demons were caged, always kept at bay,
I would abandon my needs and wants in place of your
    confidence,
Beauty of your soul and mind dominate; it's self-love not
    pompousness.

I would lose my limbs to grow into the person you are today,
You always smile, motivate, keep your dismay and never
    complain,
I would lose what little muscle I possess to become strong,
As you, glad tidings, blessings, all credit due where it belongs.

Time after time, you think you recover and are hit with dilemmas,
One after the other,
You continue to endure it for the sake of your mother,
Your father, and everyone but yourself.

I would lose my happiness in place of your health,
Of the mind, body, and I pray God increases you in wealth,
So I want to thank you for being you and staying that way,
Because without you my life would be chaos and disarray,

I know I am selfish,
But I love you,
And I hope you feel the same.

The Sarcastic Treadmill

Hibo Deria

If only I could press my own emergency stop button,
The fat mare currently jogging my belt round and round
Would soon be flicked off into her reflection in the gym mirror.
Look at those posers queuing up to check their vile reflections.
You know my dream – it's simple. To be with my friends,
Yes, treadmills have friends: me and the chest-fly machine go
way back, we arrived on the same day,
Unpackaged at the same time.
But, instead I get put next to the one thing I don't get along with:
The 'bikes', just because they had an adjustable seat,
And a sunny spot in the window.
The cross-trainers thought they were a higher cut.
You know my dream,
To be as far away from the cross trainers as possible.
They make a fool of their humans.

Six Words

Bridget Coleman

The Future is the Past,
Again.

Coming Home

Seren Pope

The silver birch drops its shadow across my brave, injured gate.
The paint has peeled to reveal a wry smile.
I flash my glad-to-be-home smile.
The rock slides with my foot,
And the gate takes its smile away from me.
The rock has told my dog I'm home,
And he wants to burst through the door.
I remove the only obstacle in my dog's way.
The furry tongue leaps off the ground and cleans my face.
I stop him from falling back to the ground,
And together we stumble in.

Excuses

Kejti Ismail

I'll do it next week –
Promise.

Home

Megan Lange

The front door is an adventure,
The living room is a ballroom,
The sofa is a prison,
And I am its captive.

The TV is a clown,
My family is the audience,
And the cables are a jigsaw that nobody can solve.

The cat is the police,
Patrolling the front room.

The corridor is a bus stop,
The coats are its passengers,
And the boxes their chairs.

The kitchen is the feeling of a week with no food,
The fridge is a magnet,
And our stomachs are made of steel.

The cooker is the sun,
And my family are the planets that orbit around it,
And every meal time is a solar eclipse,
The washing machine is a tornado,
The washing line is the rescue squad.

The garden is a new book,

And the trampoline my favourite character,
The shed is the old house at the end of the street,
And all the shovels are ghosts.

The stairs are a mountain,
The bathroom is a clothes dump,
The sink a whirlpool and the shower is a storm.

My brother's room is a dark forest,
My sister's room is a construction site,

My bedroom is a cave,
The bed is my cloud,
The windowsill my armchair,
The bookshelf is a mystery itching to be explored.

The slanted ceiling my canvas,
And my posters are my paint,

The alarm clock is a storm on a sunny day,
And the snooze-button is the breeze that blows it all away.

Student Biographies

Sarah Adams

Writing is my way of escaping from reality. I can easily spend several hours writing and be in my own little bubble. I can forget about everything for a while. I write for myself most of the time and don't normally write for anyone else's enjoyment. If you enjoy my writing, I'm glad – if you don't, that's your loss.

Guled Ali

Writing is a way of expressing your emotion. Writing should be a passion. Writing reminds me of what I do in this world. To me, writing is showing off, as you can talk about yourself in the best way possible.

Lucy-Jane Carey

Writing lets me express what I'm thinking about. I enjoy writing, even if not many people read it, because I know someone will think the same as me. The best part is you can write anywhere as long as you have a pen and paper.

Owen Clark

Owen is twelve and smart,
Some say he has a big heart,
So he rides skates all day,
Hoping to pass time away,
He is small for his age,
His ginger hair is all the rage.

Bridget Coleman

Words are the creator of her life,
(Except for her mother, of course).
She's learnt them and forgotten them,
So she's put some of them in her poems so you can remember
    them for her.
That way she can put more interesting,
And more important things into her brain.

Hibaaq Deria

Writing was never really my interest, as I thought of it to be a piece of work and not really the piece of art that others described it to be. After hearing Owen's piece, the first time I attended the club, I was truly mesmerised, blown away in fact. I'd never thought that a piece of writing could sound so good, so original and so humorous all at the same time. Fortunately, First Story has allowed me to express myself through what I write, and if my writing brings happiness to others as well as to me, then I am even more grateful.

Hibo Deria

Writing is a great way of communicating. It is a creative platform in which I am able to express myself. By attending the programme, I have gained confidence, not only in writing but in performing, too. The rush of adrenaline I gain whilst performing is surreal and sharing my creativity is something I enjoy. Writing poetry has raised my aspirations and dreams and has made me feel that now I am able to do anything. I am truly grateful for this opportunity.

Rajdeep Dulkoan

Writing is a way that I express myself, as well as a way I can share my interests with others. The good part about writing is that there are a million words you can use, so you can express yourself in your own style.

Iman Egal

I was born in Canada and came to England. My mum has four children, including me. I started school a year after I came to England and I fell in love with language. I've been writing as a form of therapy for the past three years. I love writing with a passion.

Muna Farah

I was ambivalent about writing to begin with. I was constantly coming to contradictory conclusions until I came across the quote, 'Difficulties in your life don't come to destroy you, but help you realise your hidden potential.' This quote gave me an 'aha' moment. It doesn't matter how divergent your ideas may be, writing is a form of communication, expression and self-release. And, for that, I am grateful for the opportunities that have come my way.

Abdi Gafar

Hello my name is Abdigafar and I am fourteen years old. Writing helps me communicate to others in a completely different way. It also shows people who I am and what sort of things I am interested in. For me, the best thing about writing is when I swap my work with others so that we can help each other to progress and try different styles.

Eliab Habte

I believe writing allows you to speak with well thought-out words. Nothing is done on an impulse. Writing also allows me to write out my thoughts and then I can read them as if it is someone else's life. It gives me perspective on my life.

Kejti Ismail

Writing lets me express how I feel and it puts me in my own world. It lets me choose what I want to do, when I want to do it. I can write down my actions and feelings and make a piece of writing end how I wish it to end. Writing is a friend of mine.

Muzzi Khomusi

Muzzi is fourteen years old and studies at Babington. His faith is Islam. He says he writes because it's his weapon and one day he hopes to inspire someone.

Megan Lange

Her name's Megan,
But you can call her Maagoo,
She tries not to blink,
In the presence of statues,
Maths, reading and schoolwork,
All come easily to her,
Writing, manga, drawing, books, toast,
All these things make up her life,
[Insert witty ending here].

Nicolas Merriman

His name is Nicolas,
He's not too ridiculous,
He likes interesting books,
Gets stuck in your mind like muck,
And is also quite meticulous.

Morgan Matthews-Read

Morgan is an enthusiastic and passionate writer. He has a great deal to give and he hopes that this anthology is only the start of it.

Seren Pope

Seren wants to be a unicorn,
She wants to fly,
She wants to meet the Doctor,
She wants to never blink,
She wants to know who turned out the lights,
She wants to know who her mummy is,
She wants to do the impossible,
She wants to be herself around anyone,
She wants to stop attracting awkwardness,
She wants to stop wanting.

Simon Robinson

Writing allows me to escape into my own world, which can be
shaped and moulded into what I desire it to be. This allows me to
be creative, whilst helping me to get into a calm mindset. Any
ideas I have can be put down onto paper, and turned into pieces
of fiction and stories.

Saabirin Abdulkadir-Sayed

Writing is a way in which I can express my emotions and beliefs
freely without being judged. The most important reason I write
is because it's something I take pleasure in. One day, I hope that
my writing inspires someone. This is what I truly want to achieve,
knowing that my writing is worthwhile.

Daniella Southin

For me, writing is a way of making a universe inside our universe. It gives me the power to control the destinies of characters, imagine a world of infinite possibilities and most importantly tell a story nobody else has told. Writing myself and reading the writing of others is like an escape from the ordinary, and that is why I have a passion for writing.

Zack Thotho

My name is Zack and I like writing because it allows people to express their emotions in a creative way. It lets me show my interests and my style.

Usamah Yakub

Writing helps me express my emotions clearly. It shows how creative I am. It gets me thinking and enables me to openly talk to people and say my beliefs without hesitation. I love trying to think of clever plots that interest the reader. I enjoy making everything subtle and detailed so you can enjoy every part of the story. Writing is exciting but is a challenge, too.